MISS READ'S
Christmas Book

MISS READ'S
Christmas Book

Illustrated by Tracey Williamson

MICHAEL JOSEPH
LONDON

MICHAEL JOSEPH LTD

PUBLISHED BY THE PENGUIN GROUP
27 WRIGHTS LANE, LONDON W8 5TZ
VIKING PENGUIN INC., 375 HUDSON STREET, NEW YORK, NEW YORK 10014, USA
PENGUIN BOOKS AUSTRALIA LTD, RINGWOOD, VICTORIA, AUSTRALIA
PENGUIN BOOKS CANADA LTD, 10 ALCORN AVENUE, TORONTO, ONTARIO, CANADA M4V 3B2
PENGUIN BOOKS (NZ) LTD, 182-190 WAIRAU ROAD, AUCKLAND 10, NEW ZEALAND

PENGUIN BOOKS LTD, REGISTERED OFFICES: HARMONDSWORTH, MIDDLESEX, ENGLAND

FIRST PUBLISHED IN GREAT BRITAIN 1992

EDITED, DESIGNED AND PRODUCED BY
THE ALBION PRESS LTD
P.O. BOX 52, PRINCES RISBOROUGH, AYLESBURY, BUCKS HP17 9PR

THIS ANTHOLOGY COPYRIGHT © MISS READ 1992
ILLUSTRATIONS COPYRIGHT © TRACEY WILLIAMSON 1992
DESIGN COPYRIGHT © THE ALBION PRESS LTD 1992

INDIVIDUAL EXTRACTS COPYRIGHT © WRITERS AS NOTED
SPECIFICALLY ON PAGE 124 OF THIS BOOK,
WHICH CONSTITUTES AN EXTENSION OF THIS PAGE

TYPESETTING AND COLOUR ORIGINATION BY YORK HOUSE, LONDON
PRINTED AND BOUND IN THE NETHERLANDS BY ROYAL SMEETS OFFSET B.V., WEERT

A CIP CATALOGUE RECORD FOR THIS BOOK IS AVAILABLE FROM THE BRITISH LIBRARY

ISBN 0 7181 3662 4

THE MORAL RIGHT OF THE AUTHOR HAS BEEN ASSERTED

CONTENTS

THE NATIVITY

Unto us a child is born, unto us a son is given.

THE BIBLE *Isaiah 9*

AND IT came to pass in those days, and there went out a decree from Caesar Augustus, that all the world should be taxed.

2 (And this taxing was first made when Cyrenius was governor of Syria.)

3 And all went to be taxed, every one into his own city.

4 And Joseph also went up from Galilee, out of the city of Nazareth, into Judæa, unto the city of David, which is called Bethlehem (because he was of the house and lineage of David):

5 To be taxed with Mary his espoused wife, being great with child.

6 And so it was, that, while they were there, the days were accomplished that she should be delivered.

7 And she brought forth her first-born son, and wrapped him in swaddling clothes, and laid him in a manger; because there was no room for them in the inn.

8 And there were in the same country shepherds abiding in the field, keeping watch over their flock by night.

9 And, lo, the angel of the Lord came upon them, and the glory of the Lord shone round about them: and they were sore afraid.

10 And the angel said unto them, Fear not: for, behold, I bring you good tidings of great joy, which shall be to all people.

11 For unto you is born this day in the city of David a Saviour, which is Christ the Lord.

12 And this shall be a sign unto you; Ye shall find the babe wrapped in swaddling clothes, lying in a manger.

13 And suddenly there was with the angel a multitude of the heavenly host praising God, and saying,

14 Glory to God in the highest, and on earth peace, good will toward men.

15 And it came to pass, as the angels were gone away from them into heaven, the shepherds said one to another, Let us now go even unto Bethlehem, and see this thing which is come to pass, which the Lord hath made known unto us.

16 And they came with haste, and found Mary, and Joseph, and the babe lying in a manger.

17 And when they had seen it, they made known abroad the saying which was told them concerning this child.

18 And all they that heard it wondered at those things which were told them by the shepherds.

19 But Mary kept all these things, and pondered them in her heart.

THE BIBLE *St Luke 2*

This simple and peerless account of the Nativity is the one we all know best.

It has inspired men and women throughout the centuries, and some of the finest of the world's pictures and the world's writings have the birth of Jesus as their theme.

In the following pages I have chosen my own favourites from the general rejoicing at this season of celebration.

Of the Nativity itself, I particularly like the sheer beauty of John Milton's version.

IT WAS the Winter wild,
While the Heaven-born child,
  All meanly wrapped in the rude manger lies;
Nature in awe to him
Had doffed her gaudy trim,
  With her great Master so to sympathize:
It was no season then for her
To wanton with the Sun, her lusty Paramour.

But peaceful was the night
Wherein the Prince of light
  His reign of peace upon the earth began:
The Winds with wonder whist,
Smoothly the waters kissed,
  Whispering new joys to the mild Ocean,
Who now hath quite forgot to rave,
While Birds of Calm sit brooding on the charmèd wave.

The Shepherds on the Lawn,
Or ere the point of dawn,
   Sat simply chatting in a rustic row;
Full little thought they than
That the mighty *Pan*
   Was kindly come to live with them below;
Perhaps their loves, or else their sheep,
Was all that did their silly thoughts so busy keep.

For if such holy Song
Enwrap our fancy long,
   Time will run back, and fetch the age of gold,
And speckled vanity
Will sicken soon and die,
   And leprous sin will melt from earthly mold,
And Hell itself will pass away,
And leave her dolorous mansions to the peering day.

But see, the Virgin blest
Hath laid her Babe to rest.
   Time is our tedious Song should here have ending:
Heaven's youngest teemed Star,
Hath fixed her polished Car,
   Her sleeping Lord with handmaid lamp attending;
And all about the courtly stable,
Bright-harnessed Angels sit in order serviceable.

JOHN MILTON
Hymn on the Morning of Christ's Nativity

And in complete contrast, the limpid simplicity of Mrs Alexander's hymn known since childhood.

ONCE IN ROYAL DAVID'S CITY

Once in royal David's city
    Stood a lowly cattle shed,
Where a Mother laid her Baby
    In a manger for His bed;
Mary was that Mother mild,
Jesus Christ her little Child.

He came down to earth from Heaven
    Who is God and Lord of all,
And His shelter was a stable,
    And His cradle was a stall;
With the poor, and mean, and lowly,
Lived on earth our Saviour Holy.

And our eyes at last shall see Him,
    Through His own redeeming love,
For that Child so dear and gentle
    Is our Lord in Heav'n above;
And He leads His children on
To the place where He is gone.

Not in that poor lowly stable,
    With the oxen standing by,
We shall see Him; but in Heaven,
    Set at God's right hand on high;
When like stars His children crown'd
    All in white shall wait around.

CECIL FRANCES ALEXANDER

BEFORE THE PALING OF THE STARS

Before the paling of the stars,
　Before the winter morn,
　Before the earliest cock-crow
Jesus Christ was born:
　　Born in a stable,
　Cradled in a manger,
In the world His hands had made
　　Born a stranger.

Priest and King lay fast asleep
　In Jerusalem,
Young and old lay fast asleep
　In crowded Bethlehem:
Saint and Angel, ox and ass,
　Kept a watch together,
　Before the Christmas daybreak
　In the winter weather.

CHRISTINA ROSSETTI

A CHRISTMAS CAROL

The Christ-child lay on Mary's lap,
　　His hair was like a light.
(O weary, weary were the world,
　　But here is all aright.)

The Christ-child lay on Mary's breast,
　　His hair was like a star.
(O stern and cunning are the kings,
　　But here the true hearts are.)

The Christ-child lay on Mary's heart,
　　His hair was like a fire.
(O weary, weary is the world,
　　But here the world's desire.)

The Christ-child stood at Mary's knee,
　　His hair was like a crown,
And all the flowers looked up at him,
　　And all the stars looked down.

G. K. CHESTERTON

CHRISTMAS IS COMING

Christmas is coming, the geese are getting fat,
Please to put a penny in the old man's hat.
If you haven't got a penny, a ha'penny will do,
If you haven't got a ha'penny, God bless you.

ANON. *Beggar's rhyme*

We start thinking about Christmas when winter begins, for some overseas parcels to friends have to be posted as early as October. Prudent housewives, too, are already thinking about Christmas provender as the temperature falls.

WHEN icicles hang by the wall,
And Dick the shepherd blows his nail,
And Tom bears logs into the hall,
And milk comes frozen home in pail,
When blood is nipp'd, and ways be foul,
Then nightly sings the staring owl,
                                        To-whit!
To-who! – a merry note,
While greasy Joan doth keel the pot.

When all aloud the wind doth blow,
And coughing drowns the parson's saw,
And birds sit brooding in the snow,
And Marian's nose looks red and raw,
When roasted crabs hiss in the bowl,
Then nightly sings the staring owl,
                                        To-whit!
To-who! – a merry note,
While greasy Joan doth keel the pot.

WILLIAM SHAKESPEARE   *Love's Labour Lost*

One can see why our forefathers wanted cheering through the dark days of winter. No wonder that the festival of Christmas has been the highlight of the year, bringing feasting, fireside and fun to brighten the gloom.

I HAVE often thought, says Sir Roger, it happens very well that Christmas should fall out in the Middle of Winter.

JOSEPH ADDISON *The Spectator*

CHRISTMAS was close at hand, in all his bluff and hearty honesty; it was the season of hospitality, merriment, and open-heartedness; the old year was preparing, like an ancient philosopher, to call his friends around him, and amidst the sound of feasting and revelry to pass gently and calmly away. Gay and merry was the time, and gay and merry were at least four of the numerous hearts that were gladdened by its coming.

And numerous indeed are the hearts to which Christmas brings a brief season of happiness and enjoyment. How many families, whose members have been dispersed and scattered far and wide, in the restless struggles of life, are then reunited, and meet once again in that happy state of companionship and mutual good-will, which is a source of such pure and unalloyed delight, and one so incompatible with the cares and sorrows of the world, that the religious belief of the most civilized nations, and the rude traditions of the roughest savages, alike number it among the first joys of a future condition of existence, provided for the blest and happy! How many old recollections, and how many dormant sympathies, does Christmas time awaken!

CHARLES DICKENS *The Pickwick Papers*

DECEMBER

Glad Christmas comes, and every hearth
   Makes room to give him welcome now,
E'en want will dry its tears in mirth,
   And crown him with a holly bough;
Though tramping 'neath a winter sky,
   O'er snowy paths and rimy stiles,
The housewife sets her spinning by
   To bid him welcome with her smiles.

Each house is swept the day before,
   And windows stuck with evergreens,
The snow is besom'd from the door,
   And comfort crowns the cottage scenes.
Gilt holly, with its thorny pricks,
   And yew and box, with berries small,
These deck the unused candlesticks,
   And pictures hanging by the wall.

Neighbours resume their annual cheer,
   Wishing, with smiles and spirits high,
Glad Christmas and a happy year
   To every morning passer-by;
Milkmaids their Christmas journeys go,
   Accompanied with favour'd swain;
And children pace the crumping snow,
   To taste their granny's cake again.

The shepherd, now no more afraid,
    Since custom doth the chance bestow,
Starts up to kiss the giggling maid
    Beneath the branch of mistletoe
That 'neath each cottage beam is seen,
    With pearl-like berries shining gay;
The shadow still of what hath been,
    Which fashion yearly fades away.

The singing waits, a merry throng,
    At early morn, with simple skill,
Yet imitate the angels' song,
    And chant their Christmas ditty still;
And, mid the storm that dies and swells
    By fits, in hummings softly steals
The music of the village bells,
    Ringing round their merry peals.

When this is past, a merry crew,
    Bedeck'd in masks and ribbons gay,
The "Morris-dance", their sports renew,
    And act their winter evening play.
The clown turn'd king, for penny-praise,
    Storms with the actor's strut and swell;
And Harlequin, a laugh to raise,
    Wears his hunchback and tinkling bell.

And oft for pence and spicy ale,
  With winter nosegays pinn'd before,
The wassail-singer tells her tale,
  And drawls her Christmas carols o'er.
While prentice boy, with ruddy face,
  And rime-bepowder'd, dancing locks,
From door to door with happy pace,
  Runs round to claim his "Christmas box".

JOHN CLARE *The Shepherd's Calendar*

Much of the fun of Christmas lies in the preparations that go before the great festival. As well as the catering arrangements, there are such activities as decorating the streets and public buildings, our homes and churches.

Here is Mrs Beeton's recipe for Christmas Plum Pudding. She has another recipe headed "A Plain Christmas Pudding for Children", but the following is more festive.

On reading it through, I am reminded of my days as a child when I "helped" to prepare the ingredients. Raisins then had to be stoned individually, and a messy sticky job it was. Almonds had to be soaked in warm water, and their rough brown skins slipped off. Candied peel came in glistening sugary halves of fruit, which had to be sliced thinly. My reward for assistance was the lovely circles of hard sugar which came out of the candied halves of lime, orange and lemon.

27

CHRISTMAS PLUM-PUDDING

(Very Good)

INGREDIENTS – 1½ lb. of raisins, ½ lb. of currants, ½ lb. of mixed peel, ¾ lb. of bread crumbs, ¾ lb. of suet, 8 eggs, 1 wineglassful of brandy.

Mode – Stone and cut the raisins in halves, but do not chop them; wash, pick, and dry the currants, and mince the suet finely; cut the candied peel into thin slices, and grate down the bread into fine crumbs. When all these dry ingredients are prepared, mix them well together; then moisten the mixture with the eggs, which should be well beaten, and the brandy; stir well, that everything may be very thoroughly blended, and *press* the pudding into a buttered mould; tie it down tightly with a floured cloth, and boil for 5 or 6 hours. It may be boiled in a cloth without a mould, and will require the same time allowed for cooking. As Christmas puddings are usually made a few days before they are required for table, when the pudding is taken out of the pot, hang it up immediately, and put a plate or saucer underneath to catch the water that may drain from it. The day it is to be eaten, plunge it into boiling water, and keep it boiling for at least 2 hours; then turn it out of the mould, and serve with brandy-sauce. On Christmas Day a sprig of holly is usually placed in the middle of the pudding, and about a wineglassful of brandy poured round it, which, at the moment of serving, is lighted, and the pudding thus brought to table encircled in flame.

Time – 5 or 6 hours the first time of boiling; 2 hours the day it is to be served.

Average cost, 4s.

Sufficient for a quart mould for 7 or 8 persons.

Seasonable on the 25th of December, and on various festive occasions till March.

MRS BEETON *Book of Household Management*

The Reverend James Woodforde lived at Weston Longueville Parsonage, Norfolk, from May 1776 until his death in January 1803, and throughout that time, and earlier, he kept a journal.

He, too, was fond of food and was generous in his entertaining. Every year, he remembered the old people of his parish for whom he cared.

22 December, 1788

YESTERDAY being St Thomas, the poor People came to my House for their Xmas Gifts this Morning. To 56 poor People of my Parish at 6d each gave 1.8.0.

JAMES WOODFORDE *The Diary of a Country Parson*

29

Here is a glimpse of a country church at Thrush Green, where preparations for Christmas are beginning.

THE CRIB glowed at the side of the chancel steps, and piles of ivy and other evergreens waited in readiness for the ladies of the parish to put the final touches to the Christmas decorations in the next day or two . . .

Winnie Bailey had enjoyed setting up the crib at the chancel steps on the day before the carol service. She had performed this pleasant duty for more years than she could remember, usually in the company of Ella Bembridge and Dimity, but sometimes alone.

To tell the truth, she really preferred to go about her task alone. There was something very soothing about working in the solitude of the church.

MISS READ *Celebrations at Thrush Green*

The story of the infant Jesus in the manger has moved many hearts throughout the ages. Here is a fifteenth-century poem from an unknown hand.

I SING OF A MAIDEN

I sing of a maiden
   That is makeles;
King of all kings
   To her son she ches.

He came al so still
   There his mother was,
As dew in April
   That falleth on the grass.

He came al so still
   To his mother's bour,
As dew in April
   That falleth on the flour.

He came al so still
   There his mother lay,
As dew in April
   That falleth on the spray.

Mother and maiden
   Was never none but she;
Well may such a lady
   Goddes mother be.

ANON.

31

CHRISTMAS

The bells of waiting Advent ring,
    The Tortoise stove is lit again
And lamp-oil light across the night
    Has caught the streaks of winter rain
In many a stained-glass window sheen
From Crimson Lake to Hooker's Green.

The holly in the windy hedge
    And round the Manor House the yew
Will soon be stripped to deck the ledge,
    The altar, font and arch and pew,
So that villagers can say
"The Church looks nice" on Christmas Day . . .

And is it true? And is it true,
    This most tremendous tale of all,
Seen in a stained-glass window's hue,
    A Baby in an ox's stall?
The Maker of the stars and sea
Become a Child on earth for me?

And is it true? For if it is,
    No loving fingers tying strings
Around those tissued fripperies,
    The sweet and silly Christmas things,
Bath salts and inexpensive scent
And hideous tie so kindly meant,

No love that in a family dwells,
    No carolling in frosty air,
Nor all the steeple-shaking bells
    Can with this single Truth compare –
That God was Man in Palestine
And lives today in Bread and Wine.

JOHN BETJEMAN

33

IT HAPPENED in the third year before his death, that in order to excite the inhabitants of Grecio to commemorate the nativity of the Infant Jesus with great devotion, he determined to keep it with all possible solemnity; and lest he should be accused of lightness or novelty, he asked and obtained the permission of the sovereign Pontiff. Then he prepared a manger, and brought hay, and an ox and an ass to the place appointed. The brethren were summoned, the people ran together, the forest resounded with their voices, and that venerable night was made glorious by many and brilliant lights and sonorous psalms of praise. The man of God stood before the manger, full of devotion and piety, bathed in tears and radiant with joy; many Masses were said before it, and the Holy Gospel was chanted by Francis, the Levite of Christ. Then he preached to the people around of the nativity of the poor King; and being unable to utter his Name for his tenderness of his love, he called Him the Babe of Bethlehem. A certain valiant and veracious soldier, Master John of Grecio, who, for the love of Christ, had left the warfare of this world, and become a dear friend of the holy man, affirmed that he beheld an Infant marvellously beautiful sleeping in that manger, Whom the blessed Father

Francis embraced with both his arms, as if he would awake Him from sleep. This vision of the devout soldier is credible, not only by reason of the sanctity of him that saw it, but by reason of the miracles which afterwards confirmed its truth. For the example of Francis, if it be considered by the world is doubtless sufficient to excite all hearts which are negligent in the faith of Christ; and the hay of that manger, being preserved by the people, miraculously cured all diseases of cattle, and many other pestilences; God thus in all things glorifying His servant, and witnessing to the great efficacy of his holy prayers by manifest prodigies and miracles.

SAINT BONAVENTURE *Life of Saint Francis of Assisi*

35

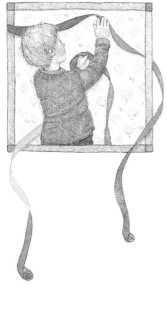

The hallowed tradition of present-giving and sending cards is one of the most important parts of the Christmas ritual. Children particularly revel in this aspect of the festivities, and enjoy getting presents ready to give away.

Here, Ernest Shepard, the distinguished artist, gives his Victorian memories.

IN THE dining-room and drawing-room our decorations were confined to holly, but Cyril and I let ourselves go in the kitchen. We had bought at Cole's, for a few pence, coloured paper streamers that opened like a concertina. By joining several together these could be hung right across the kitchen ceiling. We dragged the kitchen table from side to side and climbed on it, fixing the streamers, rather precariously, with nails and pins. However, when we had finished, and were admiring the effect, Lizzie reluctantly agreed that it did look gay. She was not much in sympathy with our activities, and wanted to know who was going to clear up the mess we had made.

I had sent off my Christmas cards: not many, but each of the Aunts had to have one; then of course Father and Mother (these were put by till tomorrow); and there were Gussie and Lizzie and her sisters. It was fortunate that I did not have to buy all these cards with my own meagre savings. Mother always kept such of last year's cards as had no writing on them, or only in pencil, and we were able to use these again. The pencil marks were erased, usually quite ineffectually, with a rather grubby piece of india-rubber, and a greeting written on top, heavily, and in ink, to help in the disguise. The procedure was fraught with dangers and I was only saved from disaster by Mother looking over my shoulder and saying, "Darling, you *can't* send that one to Aunt Alicia. It's the one she sent me last year."

ERNEST SHEPARD   *Drawn from Memory*

My generation, too, made Christmas cards when we were children. We also made bookmarks, calendars, note-pads and useful pen-wipers, now an extinct number.

As we grew older we progressed to peg-bags embroidered in lazy-daisy stitch, knitted dish-cloths and cane-and-raffia mats for putting under pot plants.

Our gifts, as I recall, were always received with gratitude and admiration. Our uncles and aunts must have been extremely well-mannered.

Mind you, we in turn received some pretty odd handmade presents. Dylan Thomas remembers some from his young days.

THERE were the Useful Presents: engulfing mufflers of the old coach days, and mittens made for giant sloths; zebra scarfs of a substance like silky gum that could be tug-o'-warred down to the galoshes; blinding tam-o'-shanters like patchwork tea cosies and bunny-suited busbies and balaclavas for victims of head-shrinking tribes; from aunts who always wore wool next to the skin there were moustached and rasping vests that made you wonder why the aunts had any skin left at all; and once I had a little crocheted nose-bag from an aunt now, alas, no longer whinnying with us. And pictureless books in which small boys, though warned with quotations not to, *would* skate on Farmer Giles' pond and did and drowned; and books that told me everything about the wasp, except why.

DYLAN THOMAS *A Child's Christmas in Wales*

It is during these days of preparation that the carol singers come.

SHORTLY after ten o'clock the singing-boys arrived at the tranter's house, which was invariably the place of meeting, and preparations were made for the start. The older men and musicians wore thick coats, with stiff perpendicular collars, and coloured handkerchiefs wound round and round the neck till the end came to hand, over all which they just showed their ears and noses, like people looking over a wall. The remainder, stalwart ruddy men and boys, were dressed mainly in snow-white smock-frocks, embroidered upon the shoulders and breasts in ornamental forms of hearts, diamonds, and zigzags. The cider-mug was emptied for the ninth time, the music-books were arranged, and the pieces finally decided upon. The boys in the meantime put the old horn-lanterns in order, cut candles into short lengths to fit the lanterns; and, a thin fleece of snow having fallen since the early part of the evening, those who had no leggings went to the stable and wound wisps of hay round their ankles to keep the insidious flakes from the interior of their boots. . .

Just before the clock struck twelve they lighted the lanterns and started. The moon, in her third quarter, had risen since the snow-storm; but the dense accumulation of snow-cloud weakened her power to a faint twilight which was rather pervasive of the landscape than traceable to the sky. The breeze had gone down, and the rustle of their feet and tones of their speech echoed with an alert rebound from every post, boundary-stone, and ancient wall they passed, even where the distance of the echo's origin was less than a few yards. Beyond their own slight noises nothing was to be heard save the occasional bark of foxes in the direction of Yalbury Wood, or the brush of a rabbit among the grass now and then as it scampered out of their way.

Most of the outlying homesteads and hamlets had been visited by about two o'clock; they then passed across the outskirts of a wooded park toward the main village, nobody being at home at the Manor. Pursuing no recognized track, great care was necessary in walking lest their faces should

come in contact with the low-hanging boughs of the old lime-trees, which in many spots formed dense overgrowths of interlaced branches.

"Times have changed from the times they used to be," said Mail, regarding nobody can tell what interesting old panoramas with an inward eye, and letting his outward glance rest on the ground because it was as convenient a position as any. "People don't care much about us now! I've been thinking we must be almost the last left in the county of the old string players? Barrel-organs, and the things next door to 'em that you blow wi' your foot, have come in terribly of late years."

"Ay!" said Bowman shaking his head; and old William on seeing him did the same thing. . .

By this time they were crossing to a gate in the direction of the school which, standing on a slight eminence at the junction of three ways, now rose in unvarying and dark flatness against the sky. The instruments were retuned, and all the band entered the school enclosure, enjoined by old William to keep upon the grass.

"Number seventy-eight," he softly gave out as they formed round in a semicircle, the boys opening the lanterns to get a clearer light, and directing their rays on the books.

Then passed forth into the quiet night an ancient and time-worn hymn, embodying a quaint Christianity in words orally transmitted from father to son through several generations down to the present characters, who sang them out right earnestly:

"Remember Adam's fall,
    O thou Man:
Remember Adam's fall
    From Heaven to Hell.
Remember Adam's fall;
How he hath condemn'd all
In Hell perpetual
    There for to dwell.

Remember God's goodnesse,
    O thou Man:
Remember God's goodnesse,
    His promise made.
Remember God's goodnesse;
He sent His Son sinlesse
Our ails for to redress;
    Be not afraid!

In Bethlehem He was born,
    O thou Man:
In Bethlehem He was born,
    For mankind's sake.
In Bethlehem He was born,
Christmas-day i' the morn:
Our Saviour thought no scorn
    Our faults to take.

Give thanks to God alway,
   O thou Man:
Give thanks to God alway
   With heart-most joy.
Give thanks to God alway
On this our joyful day:
Let all men sing and say,
   Holy, Holy!"

Having concluded the last note they listened for a minute or two, but found that no sound issued from the schoolhouse.

"Four breaths, and then, 'O, what unbounded goodness!' number fifty-nine," said William.

This was duly gone through, and no notice whatever seemed to be taken of the performance.

"Good guide us, surely 'tisn't a' empty house, as befell us in the year thirty-nine and forty-three!" said old Dewy.

"Perhaps she's jist come from some musical city, and sneers at our doings?" the tranter whispered.

" 'Od rabbit her!" said Mr Penny, with an annihilating look at a corner of the school chimney, "I don't quite stomach her, if this is it. Your plain music well done is as worthy as your other sort done bad, a' b'lieve, souls; so say I."

"Four breaths, and then the last," said the leader authoritatively. " 'Rejoice, ye Tenants of the Earth', number sixty-four."

At the close, waiting yet another minute, he said in a clear loud voice, as he had said in the village at that hour and season for the previous forty years –

"A merry Christmas to ye!"

THOMAS HARDY *Under the Greenwood Tree*

MULLED ALE

2-3 cinnamon sticks
3 blades of mace
4 cloves
1 teaspoon nutmeg
1 pint brown ale
½ teaspoon of honey
tablespoon of brandy
lemon rind

Heat ale, honey and spices, and leave for thirty minutes. Strain, reheat and pour into warm jug. Add brandy and lemon rind.

NICHOLAS CULPEPER *Herbal*

SOUNDS were heard from the fore-court without – sounds like the scuffling of small feet in the gravel and a confused murmur of tiny voices, while broken sentences reached them – "Now, all in a line – hold the lantern up a bit, Tommy – clear your throats first – no coughing after I say one, two, three. – Where's young Bill? – Here, come on, do, we're all a-waiting – "

"What's up?" inquired the Rat, pausing in his labours.

"I think it must be the field-mice," replied the Mole, with a touch of pride in his manner. "They go round carol-singing regularly at this time of the year. They're quite an institution in these parts. And they never pass me over – they come to Mole End last of all; and I used to give them hot drinks, and supper too sometimes, when I could afford it. It will be like old times to hear them again."

"Let's have a look at them!" cried the Rat, jumping up and running to the door.

It was a pretty sight, and a seasonable one, that met their eyes when they flung the door open. In the forecourt, lit by the dim rays of a horn lantern, some eight or ten little field-mice stood in a semicircle, red worsted comforters round their throats, their fore-paws thrust deep into their pockets, their feet jigging for warmth. With bright beady eyes they glanced shyly at each other, sniggering a little, sniffing and applying coat-sleeves a good deal. As the door opened, one of the elder ones that carried the lantern was just saying, "Now then, one, two, three!" and forthwith their shrill little voices uprose on the air, singing one of the old-time carols

that their forefathers composed in fields that were fallow and held by frost, or when snow-bound in chimney corners, and handed down to be sung in the miry street to lamp-lit windows at Yule-time.

CAROL

Villagers all, this frosty tide,
Let your doors swing open wide,
Though wind may follow, and snow beside,
Yet draw us in by your fire to bide;
    Joy shall be yours in the morning!

Here we stand in the cold and the sleet,
Blowing fingers and stamping feet,
Come from far away you to greet –
You by the fire and we in the street –
    Bidding you joy in the morning!

For ere one half of the night was gone,
Sudden a star had led us on,
Raining bliss and benison –
Bliss tomorrow and more anon,
    Joy for every morning!

Goodman Joseph toiled through the snow –
Saw the star o'er a stable low;
Mary she might not further go –
Welcome thatch, and litter below!
    Joy was hers in the morning!

And then they heard the angels tell
"Who were the first to cry Nowell?
Animals all, as it befell,
In the stable where they did dwell!
    Joy shall be theirs in the morning!"

The voices ceased, the singers, bashful but smiling, exchanged sidelong glances, and silence succeeded – but for a moment only. Then, from up above and far away, down the tunnel they had so lately travelled was borne to their ears in a faint musical hum the sound of distant bells ringing a joyful and clangorous peal.

"Very well sung, boys!" cried the Rat heartily. "And now come along in, all of you, and warm yourselves by the fire, and have something hot!"

KENNETH GRAHAME *The Wind in the Willows*

CHRISTMAS EVE

'Twas the night before Christmas when all through the house,
Not a creature was stirring, not even a mouse.

CLEMENT CLARKE MOORE *A Visit from St Nicholas*

ALL FAIRACRE was abustle. Margaret and Mary helped to set up the Christmas crib in the chancel of St Patrick's church. The figures of Joseph, Mary and the Child, the shepherds and the wise men reappeared every year, standing in the straw provided by Mr Roberts the farmer, and lit with sombre beauty by discreetly placed electric lights. The children came in on their way from school to see this perennial scene, and never tired of looking.

The sisters helped to decorate the church too. There were Christmas roses on the altar, their pearly beauty set off by sprigs of dark yew amidst the gleaming silver ware.

On Christmas Eve the carol singers set out on their annual pilgrimage round the village. Mr Annett, the choir master, was in charge of the church choir and any other willing chorister who volunteered to join the party . . .

One of their stopping places was outside "The Beetle and Wedge", strategically placed in the village street. Margaret and Mary opened their window and watched the singers at their work. Their breath rose in silver clouds in the light of the lanterns. The white music sheets fluttered in the icy wind which spoke of future snow to the weather-wise of Fairacre. Some of the lamps were hung on tall stout ash-sticks, and these swayed above the ruffled hair of the men and the hooded heads of the women.

Mr Annett conducted vigorously and the singing was controlled as well as robust. As the country voices carolled

the eternal story of joyous birth, Mary felt that she had never been so happy. Across the road she could see the upstairs light in the bedroom of the Emery children, and against the glowing pane were silhouetted two dark heads.

How excited they must be, thought Mary! The stockings would be hanging limply over the bed-rail, just as her own and Margaret's used to hang so many years ago. There was nothing to touch the exquisite anticipation of Christmas Eve.

> "Hark the herald angels sing,
> Glory to the new-born King,"

fluted the choir boys, their eyes on Mr Annett, their mouths like dark Os in the lamplight. And the sound of their singing rose like incense to the thousands of stars above.

MISS READ *Village Christmas*

51

THEN it was Christmas Eve, and very late at night. The moon climbed up over the roofs and chimneys, and looked down over the gateway into College Court. There were no lights in the windows, nor any sound in the houses; all the city of Gloucester was fast asleep under the snow.

When the Cathedral clock struck twelve there was an answer – like an echo of the chimes – and Simpkin heard it, and came out of the tailor's door, and wandered about in the snow.

From all the roofs and gables and old wooden houses in Gloucester came a thousand merry voices singing the old Christmas rhymes – all the old songs that ever I heard of, and some that I don't know, like Whittington's bells.

First and loudest the cocks cried out: "Dame, get up, and bake your pies!"

"Oh, dilly, dilly, dilly!" sighed Simpkin.

And now in a garret there were lights and sounds of dancing, and cats came from over the way.

"Hey, diddle, diddle, the cat and the fiddle! All the cats in Gloucester – except me," said Simpkin.

Under the wooden eaves the starlings and sparrows sang of Christmas pies; the jack-daws woke up in the Cathedral tower; and although it was the middle of the night the throstles and robins sang; the air was quite full of little twittering tunes.

BEATRIX POTTER *The Tailor of Gloucester*

24 December 1954

OH, HOW nice it would be, just for today and tomorrow, to be a little boy of five instead of an ageing playwright of fifty-five and look forward to all the high jinks with passionate excitement and be given a clockwork train with a full set of rails and a tunnel.

However, it is no use repining. As things are, drink will take the place of parlour games and we shall all pull crackers and probably enjoy ourselves enough to warrant at least some of the god-damned fuss.

NOËL COWARD *Diaries*

Christmas Eve brings children's excitement to fever-pitch. It is not only the thought of presents to come, but, even more thrilling, the magic of a visit from Father Christmas.

The mince-pie and a drink are put out for his refreshment. Sometimes chopped carrots or cornflakes are provided for his reindeer, before the child goes to bed and hangs up his stocking, secure in the knowledge that it will be filled by Father Christmas.

Later, of course, come doubts . . .

THIS HOLY NIGHT

God bless your house this holy night,
　　And all within it;

God bless the candle that you light
　　To midnight's minute:

The board at which you break your bread,
　　The cup you drink of:

And as you raise it, the unsaid
　　Name that you think of:

The warming fire, the bed of rest,
　　The ringing laughter:

These things, and all things else be blest
　　From floor to rafter

This holy night, from dark to light,
　　Even more than other;

And, if you have no house tonight,
　　God bless you, brother.

ELEANOR FARJEON

UPSTAIRS, in the double bed, the two little girls pulled the clothes to their chins and continued their day-long conversation.

A nightlight, secure in a saucer on the dressing-table, sent great shadows bowing and bending across the sloping ceiling, for the room was crisscrossed with draughts on this wild night from the ill-fitting window and door. Sometimes the brave little flame bent in a sudden blow from the cold air, as a crocus does in a gust of wind, but always it righted itself, continuing to give out its comforting light to the young children.

"Shall I tell you why I'm going to stay awake all night?" asked Jane.

"Yes."

"Promise to do what I tell you?"

"Yes."

"Promise *faithfully*? See my finger wet and dry? Cross your heart? *Everything*?"

"Everything," agreed Frances equably. Her eyelids were beginning to droop already. Left alone, free from the vehemence of her sister, she would have fallen asleep within a minute.

"Then eat your pillow," demanded Jane.

Frances was hauled back roughly from the rocking sea of sleep.

"You know I can't!" she protested.

"You promised," said Jane.

"Well, I unpromise," declared Frances. "I can't eat a

pillow, and anyway what would Mum say?"

"Then I shan't tell you what I was going to."

"I don't care," replied Frances untruthfully.

Jane, enraged by such lack of response and such wanton breaking of solemn vows, bounced over on to her side, her back to Frances.

"It was about Father Christmas," she said hotly, "but I'm not telling you now."

"He'll come," said Frances drowsily.

This confidence annoyed Jane still further.

"Maybe he won't then! Tom Williams says there isn't a Father Christmas. That's why I'm going to stay awake. To see. So there!"

Through the veils of sleep which were fast enmeshing her, Frances pondered upon this new problem. Tom Williams was a big boy, ten years old at least. What's more, he was a sort of cousin. He should know what he was talking about. Nevertheless . . .

"Tom Williams don't always speak the truth," answered Frances. In some ways, she was a wiser child than her sister.

Jane gave an impatient snort.

"Besides," said Frances, following up her point, "our teacher said he'd come. She don't tell lies. Nor Mum, nor Gran."

These were powerful allies, and Jane was conscious that Frances had some support.

"Grownups hang together," said Jane darkly. "Don't forget we saw *two* Father Christmases this afternoon in Caxley. What about that then?"

"They was men dressed up," replied Frances stolidly. "Only *pretend* Father Christmases. It don't mean there isn't a real one as 'll come tonight."

A huge yawn caught her unawares.

"You stay awake if you want to," she murmured, turning her head into the delicious warmth of the uneaten pillow. "I'm going to sleep."

Secure in her faith, she was asleep in five minutes, but Jane, full of doubts and resentful of her sister's serenity, threw her arms above her head, and, gripping the rails of the brass bedstead, grimly began her vigil. Tonight she would learn the truth!

MISS READ *The Christmas Mouse*

CHRISTMAS STOCKING

What will go into the Christmas Stocking
While the clock on the mantelpiece goes tick-tocking?
    An orange, a penny,
    Some sweets, not too many,
    A trumpet, a dolly,
    A sprig of green holly,
    A book and a top,
    And a grocery shop,
    Some beads in a box,
    An ass and an ox,
    And a lamb, plain and good,
    All whittled in wood,
    A white sugar dove,
    A handful of love,
    Another of fun,
    And it's very near done –
    A big silver star
    On top – there you are!
Come morning you'll wake to the clock's tick-tocking,
And that's what you'll find in the Christmas Stocking.

ELEANOR FARJEON

58

THE OXEN

Christmas Eve, and twelve of the clock.
"Now they are all on their knees,"
An elder said as we sat in a flock
By the embers in hearthside ease.

We pictured the meek mild creatures where
They dwelt in their strawy pen,
Nor did it occur to one of us there
To doubt they were kneeling then.

So fair a fancy few would weave
In these years! Yet, I feel,
If someone said on Christmas Eve,
"Come; see the oxen kneel

"In the lonely barton by yonder coomb
Our childhood used to know,"
I should go with him in the gloom,
Hoping it might be so.

THOMAS HARDY

CHRISTMAS DAY

At Christmas play and make good cheer
For Christmas comes but once a year.

THOMAS TUSSER

The world awakes early on Christmas morning, particularly for parents with young children who are aroused in the small hours by stone-cold feet being thrust into their beds, and the lumpy contents of Christmas stockings falling around them.

Housewives, anxious about the Christmas dinner, hasten to dress.

At Bewdley, Worcestershire, it was the custom for the bellman to go round on Christmas morning, ringing his bell and singing the following doggerel, first saying, "Good morning, masters and mistresses all, I wish you all a merry Christmas."

ARISE, mistress arise,
And make your tarts and pies,
And let your maids lie still;
For if they should rise and spoil your pies
You'd take it very ill.
Whilst you are sleeping in your bed,
I the cold wintry nights must tread,
Past twelve o'clock. Ehe!

ANON. *Worcestershire rhyme*

Bellringers are assembling ready to ring out the first joyous peal, and churchgoers are getting ready for early service.

Everywhere clergymen of every denomination are preparing for a busy day of celebration.

On Christmas Day 1870, a young curate called Robert Francis Kilvert wrote this entry in his diary.

Sunday, Christmas Day, 1870

AS I LAY awake praying in the early morning I thought I heard a sound of distant bells. It was an intense frost. I sat down in my bath upon a sheet of thick ice which broke in the middle into large pieces whilst sharp points and jagged edges stuck all round the sides of the tub like chevaux de frise, not particularly comforting to the naked thighs and loins, for the keen ice cut like broken glass. The ice water stung and scorched like fire. I had to collect the floating pieces of ice and pile them on a chair before I could use the sponge and then I had to thaw the sponge in my hands for it was a mass of ice. The morning was most brilliant. Walked to the Sunday School with Gibbins and the road sparkled with millions of rainbows, the seven colours gleaming in every glittering point of hoar frost. The Church was very cold in spite of two roaring stove fires. Mr V. preached and went to Bettws.

FRANCIS KILVERT *Diary, 1870–1879*

WAKING up on Christmas morning in childhood is something that can never be forgotten. First I was conscious of something different about the day, then I remembered, and crawled to the bottom of the bed. It was all right! The stocking was full! I fumbled in the dark and turned out one thing after another. Some were done up in paper. There were crackers and an orange, and an exciting hard box which promised chocolates. I called to Cyril and found he too was exploring in the dark. Then he boldly got out of bed and lit the gas, standing on a chair. This was not allowed, but we felt that on Christmas morning it was different. We laid all our gifts on the bed and opened the chocolates.

Presently we heard the sound of movement downstairs, and Martha came in. We shouted "Happy Christmas" but she was shocked at the gas, and said, "You know what your Father told you!" We tried to pacify her with chocolates, but the only result was for her to tell us to put them away, else we'd make ourselves sick. We got into our dressing-gowns and went down to Ethel's room. She was sitting up in bed and feeling as excited over her stocking as we were over ours.

Then we remembered about singing, and went and stood outside Mother's room and sang her a Christmas carol. She came to the door and we all hugged her and wished her a happy Christmas. After we were dressed, Cyril and I hurried downstairs to arrange our cards and little gifts on Mother's and Father's plates, and to gaze in anticipation at the sideboard piled high with parcels. Then we went to the kitchen to greet Lizzie and to tie a ribbon on Sambo; we did not stay long, for Lizzie was already busy making preparations for Christmas Dinner.

After breakfast we all opened our parcels. There were no really exciting ones for Cyril and me, as we had only just had our birthdays, but I got half a crown from Father. Then we wrapped ourselves up, for it was a foggy morning, with white hoar-frost on the trees and railings, and walked to Marylebone Church for morning Service.

E.H. SHEPARD *Drawn from Memory*

ON CHRISTMAS morning I used to wake up in the dark and smell the oranges and feel my presents, and guess at them and begin an apple and go on to sweets, especially those contained in a cardboard box scented curiously, loaf-shaped, and coloured like a top of a bun, which came from a cousin of my mother's at the Much Birch Vicarage.

EDWARD THOMAS

I have no doubt that at Marylebone Church that morning, as in many churches up and down the country, that most joyful of Christmas hymns was sung.

CHRISTIANS, AWAKE, SALUTE THE HAPPY MORN

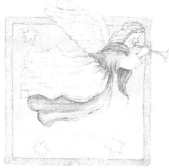

Christians, awake, salute the happy morn,
Whereon the Saviour of the world was born;
Rise to adore the mystery of love,
Which hosts of Angels chanted from above;
With them the joyful tidings first begun
Of God Incarnate and the Virgin's Son.

O may we keep and ponder in our mind
God's wondrous love in saving lost mankind;
Trace we the Babe, Who hath retrieved our loss,
From His poor manger to His bitter Cross;
Tread in His steps, assisted by His grace,
Till man's first heavenly state again takes place.

Then may we hope, the Angelic hosts among,
To sing, redeem'd, a glad triumphal song:
He that was born upon this joyful day
Around us all His glory shall display;
Saved by His love, incessant we shall sing
Eternal praise to Heav'n's Almighty King.

JOHN BYROM

GOOD master and mistress,
We wish you good cheer;
For this is old Christmas
A merry time of the year,
When Christ did come to save us
From all our worldly sin,
We wish you a happy Christmas,
And all good health within.

ANON. *Lancashire Christmas rhyme*

There were often more parcels to unwrap after returning from church.

Unexpected presents from Christmas Day visitors can pose a problem for those who have nothing ready to give in return.

A.A. Milne has a helpful suggestion.

AND NOW I am reminded of the ingenuity of a friend of mine, William by name, who arrived at a large country house for Christmas without any present in his bag. He had expected neither to give nor to receive anything, but to his horror he discovered on the 24th that everybody was preparing a Christmas present for him, and that it was taken for granted that he would require a little privacy and brown paper on Christmas Eve for the purpose of addressing his own offerings to others. He had wild thoughts of telegraphing to London for something to be sent down, and spoke to other members of the house-party in order to discover what sort of presents would be suitable.

"What are you giving our host?" he asked one of them.

"Mary and I are giving him a book," said John, referring to his wife.

William then approached the youngest son of the house, and discovered that he and his next brother Dick were sharing in this, that, and the other. When he had heard this, William retired to his room and thought profoundly.

He was the first down to breakfast on Christmas morning. All the places at the table were piled high with presents. He looked at John's place. The top parcel said, "To John and

Mary from Charles". William took out his fountain-pen and added a couple of words to the inscription. It then read, "To John and Mary from Charles and William", and in William's opinion looked just as effective as before. He moved on to the next place. "To Angela from Father", said the top parcel. "And William", wrote William. At his hostess' place he hesitated for a moment. The first present there was for "Darling Mother, from her loving children". It did not seem that an "and William" was quite suitable. But his hostess was not to be deprived of William's kindly thought; twenty seconds later the handkerchiefs "from John and Mary and William" expressed all the nice things which he was feeling for her. He passed on to the next place. . .

It is, of course, impossible to thank every donor of a joint gift; one simply thanks the first person whose eye one happens to catch. Sometimes William's eye was caught, sometimes not. But he was spared all embarrassment; and I can recommend his solution of the problem with perfect confidence to those who may be in a similar predicament next Christmas.

A.A. MILNE *If I May*

Christmas is a time for visiting and being visited. Dylan Thomas remembers some of his family's Christmas visitors.

SOME few large men sat in the front parlours, without their collars, Uncles almost certainly, trying their new cigars, holding them out judiciously at arms' length, returning them to their mouths, coughing, then holding them out again as though waiting for the explosion; and some few small Aunts, not wanted in the kitchen, nor anywhere else for that matter, sat on the very edges of their chairs, poised and brittle, afraid to break, like faded cups and saucers.

DYLAN THOMAS *A Child's Christmas in Wales*

Before long, the results of the frenzied activity in the kitchen would appear on the dinner table.

FOR DINNER we had turkey and blazing pudding, and after dinner the Uncles sat in front of the fire, loosened all buttons, put their large moist hands over their watch chains, groaned a little and slept. Mothers, aunts and sisters scuttled to and fro, bearing tureens. Auntie Bessie, who had already been frightened, twice, by a clock-work mouse, whimpered at the sideboard and had some elderberry wine. The dog was sick. Auntie Dosie had to have three aspirins, but Auntie Hannah, who liked port, stood in the middle of the snowbound back yard, singing like a big-bosomed thrush. I would blow up balloons to see how big they would blow up to; and, when they burst, which they all did, the Uncles jumped and rumbled. In the rich and heavy afternoon, the Uncles breathing like dolphins and the snow descending, I would sit among festoons and Chinese lanterns and nibble dates and try to make a model man-o'-war, following the Instructions for Little Engineers, and produce what might be mistaken for a sea-going tramcar.

DYLAN THOMAS *A Child's Christmas in Wales*

71

The best-known and best-loved description of a Christmas dinner comes from Charles Dickens in A Christmas Carol, *when the Cratchit family are celebrating at home.*

SUCH a bustle ensued that you might have thought a goose the rarest of all birds; a feathered phenomenon, to which a black swan was a matter of course – and in truth it was something very like it in that house. Mrs Cratchit made the gravy (ready beforehand in a little saucepan) hissing hot; Master Peter mashed the potatoes with incredible vigour; Miss Belinda sweetened up the apple-sauce; Martha dusted the hot plates; Bob took Tiny Tim beside him in a tiny corner at the table; the two young Cratchits set chairs for everybody, not forgetting themselves, and mounting guard upon their posts, crammed spoons into their mouths, lest they should shriek for goose before their turn came to be helped. At last the dishes were set on, and grace was said. It was succeeded by a breathless pause, as Mrs Cratchit, looking slowly all along the carving-knife, prepared to plunge it in the breast; but when she did, and when the long expected gush of stuffing issued forth, one murmur of delight arose all round the board, and even Tiny Tim, excited by the two young

Cratchits, beat on the table with the handle of his knife, and feebly cried "Hurrah!"

There never was such a goose. Bob said he didn't believe there ever was such a goose cooked. Its tenderness and flavour, size and cheapness, were the themes of universal admiration. Eked out by apple-sauce and mashed potatoes, it was a sufficient dinner for the whole family; indeed, as Mrs Cratchit said with great delight (surveying one small atom of a bone upon the dish), they hadn't ate it all at last! Yet every one had had enough, and the youngest Cratchits in particular were steeped in sage and onion to the eyebrows! But now, the plates being changed by Miss Belinda, Mrs Cratchit left the room alone – too nervous to bear witnesses – to take the pudding up and bring it in.

Suppose it should not be done enough! Suppose it should break in turning out! Suppose somebody should have got over the wall of the back-yard, and stolen it, while they were merry with the goose – a supposition at which the two young Cratchits became livid! All sorts of horrors were supposed.

Hallo! A great deal of steam! The pudding was out of the copper. A smell like a washing-day! That was the cloth. A smell like an eating-house and a pastrycook's next door to each other, with a laundress's next door to that! That was the pudding! In half a minute Mrs Cratchit entered – flushed, but smiling proudly – with the pudding, like a speckled cannon-ball, so hard and firm, blazing in half of half-a-quartern of ignited brandy, and bedight with Christmas holly stuck into the top.

Oh, a wonderful pudding! Bob Cratchit said, and calmly too, that he regarded it as the greatest success achieved by Mrs Cratchit since their marriage. Mrs Cratchit said that now the weight was off her mind, she would confess she had had her doubts about the quantity of flour. Everybody had something to say about it, but nobody said or thought it was at all a small pudding for a large family. It would have been flat heresy to do so. Any Cratchit would have blushed to hint at such a thing.

At last the dinner was all done, the cloth was cleared, the hearth swept, and the fire made up. The compound in the jug being tasted, and considered perfect, apples and oranges were put upon the table, and a shovel-full of chestnuts on the fire. Then all the Cratchit family drew round the hearth, in what Bob Cratchit called a circle, meaning half a one; and at Bob Cratchit's elbow stood the family display of glass. Two tumblers, and a custard-cup without a handle.

These held the hot stuff from the jug, however, as well as golden goblets would have done; and Bob served it out with beaming looks, while the chestnuts on the fire sputtered and cracked noisily. Then Bob proposed:

"A Merry Christmas to us all, my dears. God bless us!"

Which all the family re-echoed.

"God bless us every one!" said Tiny Tim, the last of all.

CHARLES DICKENS *A Christmas Carol*

O COME, ALL YE FAITHFUL

O come, all ye faithful,
Joyful and triumphant,
O come ye, O come ye to Bethlehem.
Come and behold him,
Born the King of Angels.

Sing, choirs of angels,
Sing in exultation,
Sing, all you citizens of heaven above;
Glory to God
In the highest.

Yea, Lord, we greet thee,
Born this happy morning,
Jesu, to thee be glory given;
Word of the Father,
Now in flesh appearing:

O come let us adore him,
O come let us adore him,
O come let us adore him,
Christ the Lord.

JOHN FRANCIS WADE

Sunday, Christmas Day, 1796

THIS being Christmas Day the following People had their Dinner at my House. Widow Case, Old Thomas Atterton, Christ. Dunnell, Edward Howes, Robert Downing and my Clerk Thos. Thurston. Dinner today surloin of Beef rosted, plumb Pudding and mince Pies. My Appetite this very cold Weather very bad. The Cold pierces me thro' almost on going to bed, cannot get to sleep for a long time, We however do not have our beds warmed. Gave the People that dined here to day before they went, to each of them 1. Shilling 0.6.0. After they had dined they had some strong Beer.

JAMES WOODFORDE *The Diary of a Country Parson*

PUT OUT the lights now!
Look at the Tree, the rough tree dazzled
In oriole plumes of flame,
Tinselled with twinkling frost fire, tasselled
With stars and moons – the same
That yesterday hid in the spinney and had no fame
Till we put out the lights now.

C. DAY LEWIS *The Christmas Tree*

Eric Newby, the eminent traveller and writer, was nineteen when he joined the crew of a four-masted barque in 1938. It was a Finnish ship, making the round trip from Belfast to Australia and back.

Here he writes of his first Christmas at sea.

FROM the midships fo'c'sle came the sound of a Christmas hymn being sung rather well in Swedish and we all went to listen. The singers were seated with their backs to the bulkhead near the Christmas tree which "Doonkey" had made from teased-out rope yarns. There were five of them sharing three hymn books and they all sang with great earnestness. Among them were Kisstar the Carpenter, the light of the oil-lamp softening the deep lines on his face; Reino Hörglund with his great black beard; and Jansson, thick-lipped and tousled. Half of the fo'c'sle was in shadow and I stood in darkness by the huge trunk of the main-mast; next to me stood Yonny Valker, hands clasped before him like a peasant before a roadside altar. We were all very homesick.

At nine o'clock we queued up outside the Captain's stateroom to receive our Christmas presents from the Missions to Seamen. This was the first time I had seen the Officers' quarters, which seemed very warm and substantial compared with our own. From somewhere the almost legendary wireless was emitting dance music with the background of peculiar rushing and whining sounds that accompany music across great expanses of ocean. . .

When it was my turn to enter the "Great Hall" I felt very serf-like and nervous, but my premonitions were soon dispersed. Inside it was all red plush, banquettes, and brass rails, very like the old Café Royal. I almost expected to see Epstein instead of the smiling and very youthful-looking Captain seated at the mahogany table, his officers around him. He held out a hat to me, full of pieces of paper. The one I took was Number 7. "Number 7 for England's Hope," said the Captain, and the Steward who was kneeling on the floor surrounded by parcels handed me the one with 7 on it. I wished everybody "God Jul" and backed out of the stateroom in fine feudal fashion, stepping heavily on the toes of the man behind me, and dashed eagerly back to the fo'c'sle to open it.

Inside the paper wrappings was a fine blue knitted scarf, a pair of grey mittens, and a pair of stout brown socks. When I picked up the scarf three bits of paper fell out. One of these was a Christmas card with "Jultiden" in prominent red lettering on one side and on the other, in ink, "och Gott Nytt År, onskar Aina Karlsson, Esplanadgarten 8, Mariehamn." On the other two pieces was the text of St John, Chapter 20, in

Finnish, and the good wishes of the Missions to Seamen who had sent the parcel. Right at the bottom was a hand mirror and comb.

I thought of Aina Karlsson knitting woollies with loving care for unknown sailors in sailing ships. We all eagerly compared our presents. Some had thicker garments, some larger. Sedelquist said that the Mates had already appropriated the best, but no one paid any attention to this. Among us Taanila had the finest haul – a woollen helmet that pulled over head and ears with a long scarf attached. It made him look like a fiendish Finnish gnome . . .

I went in search of my bunk. It was 9.45. By some miracle I was neither "rorsman", "utkik", nor "påpass". I crawled into my bag and slept dreamlessly until four in the morning, when a voice cried "resa upp"; but Sandell closed the curtains and I slept on until half past seven. There were loud cheers when I woke. I had slept "like sonofabeetch, like peeg in straw." Ten hours – the longest sleep I ever had in *Moshulu*, or anywhere else. I was quite thrilled.

On Christmas morning the weather was cold and brilliant. Big following seas were charging up astern in endless succession. They surged beneath the ship, bearing her up, filling the air with whistling spray as their great heads tore out from under and ahead to leave her in a trough as black and polished as basalt except where, under the stern post, the angle of the rudder made the water bubble jade-green, as if from a spring. From the mizzen yardarm, where I hung festooned with photographic apparatus, I could see the whole midships of *Moshulu*. On the flying bridge above the main deck the Captain and the three Mates were being photographed by the Steward, solemn and black as crows in their best uniforms.

Rigid with cold I descended to eat Christmas dinner, for which the "Kock" had made an extra sustaining fruit soup. For breakfast we had had Palethorpe's tinned sausages which were very well received; at "Coffee-time" apple tarts and buns but not enough of either; and for supper, rice, pastry, and jam. At four a.m. on what would have been Boxing Day in England we were setting royals once more. The party was over.

ERIC NEWBY *The Last Grain Race*

On Christmas afternoon most people feel the need for exercise, even if it is only a short walk. Some, of course, are more energetic, as Mr Pickwick and his friends were on one distant Christmas afternoon.

"Now," said Wardle, after a substantial lunch, with the agreeable items of strong beer and cherry-brandy, had been done ample justice to; "what say you to an hour on the ice? We shall have plenty of time."

"Capital!" said Mr Benjamin Allen.

"Prime!" ejaculated Mr Bob Sawyer.

"You skate, of course, Winkle?" said Wardle.

"Ye-yes; oh, yes," replied Mr Winkle. "I – I – am *rather* out of practice."

"Oh, *do* skate, Mr Winkle," said Arabella. "I like to see it so much."

"Oh, it is *so* graceful," said another young lady.

A third young lady said it was elegant, and a fourth expressed her opinion that it was "swan-like".

"I should be very happy, I'm sure," said Mr Winkle, reddening; "but I have no skates."

This objection was at once overruled. Trundle had a couple of pair, and the fat boy announced that there were half-a-dozen more down stairs: whereat Mr Winkle expressed exquisite delight, and looked exquisitely uncomfortable.

Old Wardle led the way to a pretty large sheet of ice; and the fat boy and Mr Weller, having shovelled and swept away the snow which had fallen on it during the night, Mr Bob Sawyer adjusted his skates with a dexterity which to Mr Winkle was perfectly marvellous, and described circles with his left leg, and cut figures of eight, and inscribed upon the ice, without once stopping for breath, a great many other pleasant and astonishing devices, to the excessive satisfaction of Mr Pickwick, Mr Tupman, and the ladies: which reached a pitch of positive enthusiasm, when old Wardle and Benjamin Allen, assisted by the aforesaid Bob Sawyer, performed some mystic evolutions, which they called a reel.

All this time, Mr Winkle, with his face and hands blue with the cold, had been forcing a gimlet into the soles of his feet, and putting his skates on, with the points behind, and getting the straps into a very complicated and entangled state, with the assistance of Mr Snodgrass, who knew rather less about skates than a Hindoo. At length, however, with the assistance of Mr Weller, the unfortunate skates were firmly screwed and buckled on, and Mr Winkle was raised to his feet.

"Now, then, sir," said Sam, in an encouraging tone; "off vith you, and show 'em how to do it."

"Stop, Sam, stop!" said Mr Winkle, trembling violently, and clutching hold of Sam's arms with the grasp of a drowning man. "How slippery it is, Sam!"

"Not an uncommon thing upon ice, sir," replied Mr Weller. "Hold up, sir!"

This last observation of Mr Weller's bore reference to a demonstration Mr Winkle made at the instant, of a frantic desire to throw his feet in the air, and dash the back of his head on the ice.

"These – these – are very awkward skates; ain't they, Sam?" inquired Mr Winkle, staggering.

"I'm afeerd there's a orkard gen'l'm'n in 'em, sir," replied Sam.

"Now, Winkle," cried Mr Pickwick, quite unconscious that there was anything the matter. "Come; the ladies are all anxiety."

"Yes, yes," replied Mr Winkle, with a ghastly smile. "I'm coming."

"Just a goin' to begin," said Sam, endeavouring to disengage himself. "Now, sir, start off!"

"Stop an instant, Sam," gasped Mr Winkle, clinging most affectionately to Mr Weller. "I find I've got a couple of coats at home that I don't want, Sam. You may have them, Sam."

"Thank'ee sir," replied Mr Weller.

"Never mind touching your hat, Sam," said Mr Winkle, hastily. "You needn't take your hand away to do that. I meant to have given you five shillings this morning for a Christmas-box, Sam. I'll give it you this afternoon, Sam."

"You're wery good, sir," replied Mr Weller.

"Just hold me at first, Sam; will you?" said Mr Winkle. "There – that's right. I shall soon get in the way of it, Sam. Not too fast, Sam; not too fast."

Mr Winkle stooping forward, with his body half doubled up, was being assisted over the ice by Mr Weller, in a very singular and un-swan-like manner, when Mr Pickwick most innocently shouted from the opposite bank:

"Sam!"

"Sir?"

"Here. I want you."

"Let go, sir," said Sam. "Don't you hear the governor a callin'? Let go, sir."

With a violent effort, Mr Weller disengaged himself from the grasp of the agonised Pickwickian, and, in so doing, administered a considerable impetus to the unhappy Mr Winkle. With an accuracy which no degree of dexterity or practice could have insured, that unfortunate gentleman bore swiftly down into the centre of the reel, at the very moment when Mr Bob Sawyer was performing a flourish of unparalleled beauty. Mr Winkle struck wildly against him, and with a loud crash they both fell heavily down. Mr Pickwick ran to the spot. Bob Sawyer had risen to his feet, but Mr Winkle was far too wise to do anything of the kind, in skates. He was seated on the ice, making spasmodic efforts to smile; but anguish was depicted on every lineament of his countenance.

"Are you hurt?" inquired Mr Benjamin Allen, with great anxiety.

"Not much," said Mr Winkle, rubbing his back very hard.

"I wish you'd let me bleed you," said Mr Benjamin, with great eagerness.

"No, thank you," replied Mr Winkle hurriedly.

"I really think you had better," said Allen.

"Thank you," replied Mr Winkle; "I'd rather not."

"What do *you* think, Mr Pickwick?" inquired Bob Sawyer.

Mr Pickwick was excited and indignant. He beckoned to Mr Weller, and said in a stern voice, "Take his skates off."

"No; but really I had scarcely begun," remonstrated Mr Winkle.

"Take his skates off," repeated Mr Pickwick firmly.

The command was not to be resisted. Mr Winkle allowed Sam to obey it in silence.

"Lift him up," said Mr Pickwick. Sam assisted him to rise.

Mr Pickwick retired a few paces apart from the by-standers; and, beckoning his friend to approach, fixed a searching look upon him, and uttered in a low, but distinct and emphatic tone, these remarkable words:

"You're a humbug, sir."

"A what?" said Mr Winkle, starting.

"A humbug, sir. I will speak plainer, if you wish it. A impostor, sir."

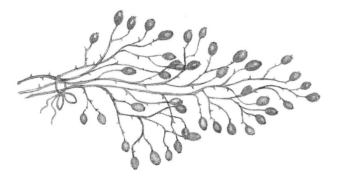

With those words, Mr Pickwick turned slowly on his heel, and rejoined his friends.

CHARLES DICKENS *The Pickwick Papers*

This emphasis on the cold weather at Christmas time is all part of its magic. Snow plays a large part, ice and frost abound. Santa Claus has to go about his duties by sledge, and most of our Christmas cards depict snowy scenes.

IN THE bleak mid-winter
Frosty wind made moan,
Earth stood hard as iron,
Water like a stone;
Snow had fallen, snow on snow,
Snow on snow,
In the bleak mid-winter,
Long ago.

Our God, heav'n cannot hold him
Nor earth sustain;
Heav'n and earth shall flee away
When he comes to reign:
In the bleak mid-winter
A stable-place sufficed
The Lord God Almighty
Jesus Christ.

Enough for him, whom cherubim
Worship night and day,
A breastful of milk,
And a mangerful of hay;
Enough for him, Whom angels
Fall down before,
The ox and ass and camel
Which adore.

Angels and Archangels
May have gathered there,
Cherubim and Seraphim
Thronged the air:
But only his mother
In her maiden bliss
Worshipped the Beloved
With a kiss.

What can I give him,
Poor as I am?
If I were a shepherd
I would bring a lamb;
If I were a wise man
I would do my part;
Yet what can I give him –
Give my heart.

CHRISTINA ROSSETTI

It is no wonder that, "in the bleak mid-winter", when we celebrate Christmas, the fireside, family, friends and fun take precedence as night falls.

It is only fair though to point out that the few days around Christmas Day are often extremely mild, and in fact there have only been seven white Christmases recorded in London since 1900.

Nevertheless, after dark the festivities concentrate in the home.

Here Dylan Thomas remembers the end of one childhood Christmas Day.

ALWAYS on Christmas night there was music. An uncle played the fiddle, a cousin sang "Cherry Ripe", and another uncle sang "Drake's Drum". It was very warm in the little house.

Auntie Hannah, who had got on to the parsnip wine, sang a song about Bleeding Hearts and Death, and then another in which she said her heart was like a Bird's Nest; and then everybody laughed again; and then I went to bed. Looking through my bedroom window, out into the moonlight and the unending smoke-coloured snow, I could see the lights in the windows of all the other houses on our hill and hear the music rising from them up the long, steadily falling night. I turned the gas down, I got into bed. I said some words to the close and holy darkness, and then I slept.

DYLAN THOMAS *A Child's Christmas in Wales*

In contrast, here are an old man's reflections on Christmas.

Christmas Day, 1918

THIS morning was typical Christmas weather, a white frost and a brilliant sky. I have been to a children's party at Dolly's where we played games. It was happy and yet sad to an old man. One remembers so many Christmas parties as far back as fifty years and more ago and oh! where are the children that played at them? There is a tall oak clock ticking away at the end of this room; the man who cleaned it the other day said it was the oldest he had ever handled. It has seen many more Christmasses than I have, four or five times the number, and still it ticks unconcernedly, marking the passage of the hours and the years. Doubtless it sounded the moment of my birth as it will do that of my death. Remorselessly it ticks on, counting the tale of the fleeting moments from Yule to Yule. Yes, Christmas is a sad feast for the old, and yet – thanks be to God who giveth us the victory – one is full of hope.

SIR HENRY RIDER HAGGARD *Diary 1914–1925*

But amidst the glow of Christmas and goodwill of man to man, there are inevitably those who suffer.

Francis Kilvert has a sombre entry for Christmas Day 1878.

Wednesday, Christmas Day, 1878

VERY hard frost last night. At Presteign the thermometer fell to 2 degrees, showing 30 degrees of frost. At Monnington it fell to 4. Last night is said to have been the coldest night for 100 years. The windows of the house and Church were so thick with frost rime that we could not see out. We could not look through the Church windows all day. Snow lay on the ground and the day was dark and gloomy with a murky sky. A fair morning congregation considering the weather. By Miss Newton's special desire Dora and I went to the Cottage to eat our Christmas dinner at 1.30 immediately after service.

Immediately after dinner I had to go back to the church for the funeral of little Davie of the Old Weston who died on Monday was fixed for 2.15. The weather was dreadful, the snow driving in blinding clouds and the walking tiresome. Yet the funeral was only 20 minutes late. The Welcome Home, as it chimed softly and slowly to greet the little pilgrim coming to his rest, sounded bleared and muffled through the thick snowy air. The snow fell thickly all through the funeral service and at the service by the grave a kind woman offered her umbrella which a kind young fellow came and held over my head. The woman and man were Mrs Richards and William Jackson. I asked the poor mourners to come in and rest and warm themselves but they would not and went into Church. The poor father, David Davies the shepherd, was crying bitterly for the loss of his little lamb. Owing to the funeral it was rather late before we began the afternoon service. There were very few people in Church beside the mourners. The afternoon was very dark. I was obliged to move close to the great south window to read the Lessons and could hardly see even then. I preached from Luke ii.7. "There was no room for them in the inn", and connected the little bed in the churchyard in which we had laid Davie to rest with the manger cradle at Bethlehem.

In spite of the heavy and deep snow there was a fair congregation at Brobury Church. I walked there with Powell. The water was out in Brobury lane. As we came back a thaw had set in and rain fell. By Miss Newton's special wish I went to the Cottage and spent the evening with Dora. The Cottage servants had invited the Vicarage servants to tea and supper and they came into the drawing-room after supper and sang some Christmas Carols.

FRANCIS KILVERT *Diary 1870–1879*

The passage is doubly poignant for that was Francis Kilvert's last Christmas.

In the following year, in August 1879, he married Elizabeth Anne Rowland, at the lovely church of Wooton near Woodstock, Oxfordshire, and took his bride back to Bredwardine, close to his beloved Clyro.

A month later, he died of peritonitis.

THE HOLLY AND THE IVY

The holly and the ivy,
When they are both full grown,
Of all the trees that are in the wood,
The holly bears the crown:

The rising of the sun
And the running of the deer,
The playing of the merry organ,
Sweet singing in the choir.

The holly bears a blossom,
As white as the lily flower,
And Mary bore sweet Jesus Christ,
To be our sweet Saviour:

The rising of the sun
And the running of the deer,
The playing of the merry organ,
Sweet singing in the choir.

The holly bears a berry,
As red as any blood,
And Mary bore sweet Jesus Christ,
To do poor sinners good:

The rising of the sun
And the running of the deer,
The playing of the merry organ,
Sweet singing in the choir.

The holly bears a prickle,
As sharp as any thorn,
And Mary bore sweet Jesus Christ
On Christmas day in the morn:

The rising of the sun
And the running of the deer,
The playing of the merry organ,
Sweet singing in the choir.

The holly bears a bark,
As bitter as any gall,
And Mary bore sweet Jesus Christ
For to redeem us all:

The rising of the sun
And the running of the deer,
The playing of the merry organ,
Sweet singing in the choir.

BOXING DAY TO TWELFTH NIGHT

Let joy be unconfined.

BYRON *Childe Harold's Pilgrimage*

The day after Christmas Day is reckoned by some people to be one of recovery from the rich living of the day before.

Certainly for most housewives it is a relief to wake to the thought of plenty of cold turkey and ham in the larder, and the welcome knowledge that catering will be minimal. The children, of course, with plenty of new presents to enjoy, greet the day with enthusiasm.

Boxing Day derives its name from the custom of giving Christmas alms to the poor of the parish from a box kept in the church for this purpose and opened on Boxing Day.

Nowadays, we present those who have been of service to us with their Christmas boxes, or tips, usually before Boxing Day. Christmas cards, suitably inscribed, together with money, are handed to the dustman, the milkman, the postman and so on, who have given their services throughout the year to the householder.

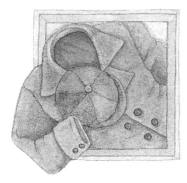

THE DAY after Christmas Day was a high day with us as Bluecoat boys. We then received our yearly new coat and cap, at the house of Dr Parnell. "Gervase Parnell, Esquire", was his full name and title; and a finer specimen of the old-fashioned gentleman, with powdered head and tail, and his gold-headed cane, you would nowhere see. When we had received our new dresses at his house, he presented us with twopence each; and then away we went in procession to collect our "Christmas-boxes". We used to begin with Mr Sandars, the corn-merchant, whose house was nearest the bridge; and then went through the town to Morton, calling at the houses of the merchants and gentry, whose names of

Furley, and Etherington, and Torr, and Morehouse, and Barnard, and Garfitt, and Flowers, and Coats, and Metcalfe, and Smith, and Dealtry, and Brightmore, are far more familiar to me, now sixty years have passed away, since I first knew them, than any names that I learned but yesterday. Our last call in the town was upon the Rev. Mr Fothergill, the vicar; and then away we went to Morton, and from Morton we sped away to Thonock Hall, the seat of old Miss Hickman, the lady of the manor, and heiress of Sir Neville George Hickman, Bart.

Money was always given to us, and, at some houses, bread and cheese and beer. I cannot say we always shared alike in what was thus kindly given; for I remember how, one severe snowy season, the big lads who carried the money-box persuaded some of us, who were weak and shivering with cold, to go home with a very few halfpence each, while they went on, and roguishly kept the larger share of the money for themselves. Fear of punishment, however, usually kept the big lads tolerably honest.

THOMAS COOPER *The Life of Thomas Cooper*

Boxing Day is a Bank Holiday, and is really the start of the days of jollity, including New Year's Eve, which end with Twelfth Night on 6 January.

Samuel Pepys enjoyed a visit to the theatre in 1668.

26 December, 1668

LAY LONG, with pleasure prating with my wife; and then up, and I a little to the office, and my head busy setting some papers and accounts to rights: which being long neglected because of my eyes, will take me up much time and care to do, but it must be done. So home at noon to dinner; and then abroad with my wife to a play at the Duke of York's House; the house full of ordinary citizens; the play was *Women pleased*, which we had never seen before; and though but indifferent, yet there is a good design for a good play. So home, and there to talk and my wife to read to me, and so to bed.

SAMUEL PEPYS *Diary*

Over two hundred years later, Ernest Shepard went to the theatre to see his first pantomime.

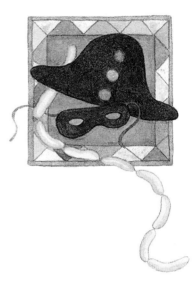

THIS was before Dan Leno's day; he did not come to Drury Lane till a year or two later. But I remember a gay young woman with prominent teeth and a flaxen wig who sang and danced bewitchingly. She could only have been Marie Lloyd, the unforgettable, aged seventeen and in her first Pantomime at "the Lane". In the Harlequinade the clown was an old favourite, Harry Payne, so Father told us, who had been clowning for years and was shortly to give place to another famous clown, Whimsical Walker.

It was all such a feast of colour, music, and fun, and it would be quite impossible to express all the emotions that were aroused in a small boy's breast. I know that I stood gripping the velvet-covered front of the box, lost in a wonderful dream, and that when the curtain fell at the end of the first act and the lights in the auditorium went up, I sat back on Mother's lap with a sigh. I could not speak when she asked me if I was enjoying the show. I could only nod my head. I did not think it possible that such feminine charms existed as were displayed by the Principal Boy. Ample-bosomed, small-waisted and with thighs – oh, such thighs! – thighs that shone and glittered in the different coloured silk tights in which she continually appeared. How she strode about the stage, proud and dominant, smacking those rounded limbs with a riding crop! At every smack, a fresh

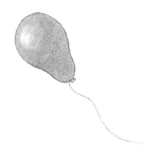

dart was shot into the heart of at least one young adorer. I had a grand feeling that it was all being done for my especial benefit: the whole performance was for *me*; the cast had all been told that they were to do their best because *I* was there. Nobody else, not even Mother, could feel exactly the same as I did.

I had one dreadful moment when I happened to look round while the adored one was singing one of her songs. . . . Father, at the back of the box, was reading a newspaper. I could hardly believe my eyes. Could it be that he was so overcome that he was trying to conceal his emotion by this show of indifference? Yes, no doubt that was it; but I have since wondered if I was right.

The spectacle reached a climax with the transformation scene. Glittering vistas appeared one behind the other, sparkling lace-like canopies spread overhead, a real fountain poured forth in the background. On either side golden brackets swung out from the wings, each with its reclining nymph, solid and spangled and in a graceful attitude. Flying fairies, poised but swaying gently, filled the air and formed a sort of triumphal archway, below which the performers gathered. The Good Fairy, stepping forward, invoked in rhymed couplets the Spirit of Pantomime, and out from the wings burst Joey the clown, Pantaloon, Columbine, and Harlequin to complete the tableau. Not quite, for, led by the Principal Boy, there came Augustus Harris himself, immaculate in evening dress with white waistcoat, to receive the plaudits of a delighted audience.

There was still the Harlequinade to come. The red-hot poker (that kept hot for a remarkably long time), the strings of sausages, the stolen goose, the Pantaloon always in difficulties, the Policeman, blown up and put together again. Oh, how I longed for it to go on for ever! Then Harlequin, with a wave of his wand, brought on his Columbine, so fair and dainty, but not so lovely as to steal one's heart, though she helped Joey to rob the shopman. On came the tall thin man who sang and sang the while he was belaboured by Joey and Pantaloon. And then – the end!

It was really over at last. No use to gaze at the dropped curtain, the dimming lights or the emptying theatre. I was speechless as we muffled up for the journey home.

ERNEST SHEPARD *Drawn from Memory*

Traditionally, there is a meet of the local hunt on Boxing Day, and here is an account of one in Suffolk in the 1930s by Adrian Bell.

WE MOUNTED and were off. Mr Colville looked a typical hunting farmer with his round face under his bowler hat. He had lent me a bowler, that I might look the part, as I had not brought one, hardly considering it applicable to country life, the possibility of hunting being a fantastic vision in Chelsea.

He rode Jock, the heavyweight, while I perched on the nimble Cantilever.

"Rare good jumper, that mare is," said Mr Colville. But the news at that time did not thrill me, only suggested a disturbing possibility of the mare springing suddenly from under me. "She's safe, too." That was better. "But don't let other horses get too near her; she might kick. Only in play, of course; but people wouldn't like it."

Apprehension again! Where did I go when she kicked?

A light wind was blowing. The mist had risen early, and the day was cold and clear. Conversation was cut short for the moment because a piece of paper in the road woke up and flapped, and the next I knew was that horse and I were on the top of a steep bank and then on the road again twenty yards ahead. I found I was still on the horse's back.

"I shouldn't let her do that," said Mr Colville blandly. "It's just that she's a bit bird-eyed, being fresh out." He added:

"But I like to see a horse show a bit of spirit."

I noticed, however, that his was a model of decorum, with complacent ears. (Cantilever's were a-twitch with nervous inquiry.) Occasionally Mr Colville would make believe Jock had stumbled, and growl at him. I began to envy him his mount, though certainly Jock had not seemed as docile under me. Mr Colville's extra weight, no doubt. Jock moved with the magisterial surety of an elephant beneath his rider's fourteen stone.

Mr Colville exclaimed: "I wish I were light enough to ride your mare. I'd show some of them how to go. Now, you're a nice weight; you could ride anything." He sighed. "Ah, well, you are only young once. I never cared what I rode one time of day, but I have to be careful now. I'm no light weight to fall."

The hounds were gathered in front of the Rose and Crown with the huntsmen and whips near by. The small space was packed with cars, horses, and people.

Everybody knew Mr Colville, and I kept alongside him. Cantilever was a-quiver with anticipation, and I had some apprehension in guiding her between shining limousines and the haunches of other horses, especially those with red tape on their tails – a danger sign of which Mr Colville had informed me.

The hounds alone were unaffected by the subdued excitement. They lay about with lolling tongues and sleepy red eyes, and occasionally yawned.

Consultations were in progress between the master and

the huntsman, a shrewd old leatherface. There came a short toot of the horn and they were moving off.

Mr Colville turned to me. "What do you think about it? Coming on or not?"

Before I could decide, I found myself swept onward in a crowd of horses. Cantilever was in no mood to retire. I went with the tide and hoped for the best.

"The only thing is," I said, "I have never done any jumping."

"The mare is as safe as a church," answered Mr Colville. "All you have to do is to sit back and hold tight. Hug her well with your legs."

I hoped my legs would be equal to the occasion. I was balanced, I felt, rather than seated.

We entered a field and spread. As soon as their feet touched soft earth, many of the horses tried to canter, and one or two bucked sensationally. I held Cantilever close, for she seemed disposed to give an exhibition of high spirits herself. Mr Colville's mount was magisterial as ever, his only sign of enthusiasm being to lift his legs higher and jog occasionally.

"We shall find here," said Mr Colville, indicating a wood ahead. "We always do."

We stood under the shadow of the trees. The whole hunt seemed to have vanished, and silence reigned. A crowd of pigeons flew out of the wood. Rabbits lolloped silently towards us, paused, and scuttled away. A hare dashed past with a swishing noise through the stubble.

"'Ark!" whispered Mr Colville, "is that a 'oller?" – his aitches forsaking him at the moment of excitement.

I listened obediently, for what kind of noise I knew not; but Cantilever continued to champ her bit restlessly. Mr Colville raised his fist at her threateningly, but I saw no means of causing her to desist.

Suddenly a yelping and roaring filled the air, which immediately flashed upon me a childhood memory of the lions waiting to be fed at the Zoo.

"Ah!" said Mr Colville, "that's the music at last."

ADRIAN BELL *Corduroy*

But not everyone had fun on Boxing Day. Here is Hannah Cullwick's account.

26 December 1863

I LIGHTED the fires & black'd the grates – the kitchen grate was so greasy I'd to wash it over first. I felt glad the Christmas was over so far for if it kept on long as it's bin the last 3 or 4 days I should be knock'd up I think. I clean'd 2 pairs o' boots. Swept & dusted the room & the hall & got the breakfast up. The Missis came down into the kitchen & look'd round at what was left, & paid me my quarter's wages. She saw I'd got a mistletoe hanging up & I told her ther'd bin no one kiss'd yet.

HANNAH CULLWICK *The Diaries of Hannah Cullwick,*
Victorian Maidservant

Festivities continue all through the days following Christmas.

27 December 1870

AFTER dinner drove into Chippenham with Perch and bought 2 pair of skates at Benk's for 17/6. Across the fields to the Draycot water and the young Awdry ladies chaffed me about my new skates. I had not been on skates since I was here last, 5 years ago, and was very awkward for the first ten minutes, but the knack soon came again. There was a distinguished company on the ice, Lady Dangan, Lord and Lady Royston and Lord George Paget all skating. Also Lord and Lady Sydney and a Mr Calcroft, whom they all of course called the Hangman. I had the honour of being knocked down by Lord Royston, who was coming round suddenly on the outside edge. A large fire of logs burning within an enclosure of wattled hurdles. Harriet Awdry skated beautifully and jumped over a half-sunken punt. Arthur Law skating jumped over a chair on its legs.

FRANCIS KILVERT *Diary 1870–1879*

Some of these celebrations date from very early times, and wassailing was one of them.

As the New Year approached, the Wassailers would call at local houses, rather as carol-singers do now, but they would carry a large bowl with them containing a spicy punch. The householder would drink from the bowl, give alms to the wassailers, and listen to their songs.

THAMES HEAD WASSAILERS' SONG

Wassail, wassail, all over the town,
Our toast is white and our ale is brown,
Our bowl it is made of a maplin tree,
And so is good beer of the best barley.

Here's to the ox, and to his long horn;
May God send our maester a good crap o' corn!
A good crap o' corn, and another o' hay,
To pass the cold wintry winds away.

Here's to the ox, and to his right ear;
May God send our maester a happy New Year!
A happy New Year, as we all may see,
With our wassailing bowl we will drink unto thee.

Here's to old Jerry, and to her right eye;
May God send our mistress a good Christmas pie!
A good Christmas pie, as we all may see,
And a wassailing bowl we will drink unto thee.

Here's to old Boxer, and to his long tail;
I hope that our maester'll hae n'er a 'oss vail!
N'er a 'oss vail, as we all may see,
And a wassailing bowl we will drink unto thee.

Come, pretty maidens – I suppose there are some!
Never let us poor young men stand on the cold stone;
The stones they are cold, and our shoes they are thin,
The fairest maid in the house let us come in!
Let us come in, and see how you do.

ANON. *Upper Thames*

WASSAIL CUP

2 3in cinnamon sticks
4 cloves
3 blades mace
1 ginger root
1 level teaspoon nutmeg

4 apples
4oz sugar
½ pint brown ale
½ pint cider

Core apples and sprinkle with sugar and water. Bake at 375°F
or gas no. 5 for 30 minutes or until tender. Mix ale, cider and
spices together. Heat but do not boil. Leave for 30 minutes.
Strain and pour over roasted apples. Serve in a punch bowl.

NICHOLAS CULPEPER *Herbal*

This is the time when the children are home from school, and there is much to-ing and fro-ing during the winter afternoons taking them to parties.

For the grown-ups the merriest party comes on New Year's Eve, when a number of traditions are honoured.

One of them is First Footing, when the first person to cross the threshold brings good luck to the household for the year to come.

There are provisions about this custom. The First Footer must be dark-haired and carry a lump of coal and a piece of bread. In some places he is also required to bring in salt and a sprig of evergreen.

New Year resolutions are made now, and as midnight strikes hands are linked and "Auld Lang Syne" is sung.

> SHOULD auld acquaintance be forgot
>   And never brought to mind?
> Should auld acquaintance be forgot,
>   And auld lang syne!
>
> *For auld lang syne, my dear,*
>   *For auld lang syne,*
> *We'll tak a cup o' kindness yet*
>   *For auld lang syne.*

ROBERT BURNS *Auld Lang Syne*

(The Scots among us presumably know what they are singing, but for us Sassenachs it is quite permissible to sing "Ol' Langzine" over and over again. The Scots, of course, are celebrating Hogmanay at the same time.)

Here are three diary entries for the last day of the year.
Samuel Pepys is writing at the end of the year of the Great Fire of London.

1666

THUS ends this year of public wonder and mischief to this nation – and therefore generally wished by all people to have an end. Myself and family well, having four maids and one clerk, Tom, in my house; and my brother now with me, to spend time in order to his preferment. Our healths all well; only, my eyes, with overworking them, are sore as soon as candlelight comes to them, and not else. Public matters in a most sad condition. Seamen discouraged for want of pay, and are become not to be governed. Nor, as matters are now, can any fleet go out next year. Our enemies, French and Duch, great, and grow more, by our poverty. The Parliament backward in raising, because jealous of the spending, of the money. The City less and less likely to be built again, everybody settling elsewhere, and nobody encouraged to trade. A sad, vicious, negligent Court, and all sober men there fearful of the ruin of the whole Kingdom this next year – from which, good God deliver us. One thing I reckon remarkable in my own condition is that I am come to abound in good plate, so as at all entertainments to be served wholly with silver plates, having two dozen and a half.

SAMUEL PEPYS *Diary*

1844

HERE ends the best & brightest & most blessed year of my life. It is as tho' I had reached the goal of my boy-existence & found it but the starting post of a new one. The mountain tops before me show higher than ever & life is become a more earnest business with a larger sphere & higher pleasures & deeper responsibilities – no longer alone but blest with the companionship of a noble & pure spirit, with the possession of a deeply loving heart; how abundantly grateful ought mine to be!

BARCLAY FOX *Journal*

1857

THE DEAR old year is gone, with all its *Weben* and *Streben*. Yet not gone either: for what I have suffered and enjoyed in it remains to me an everlasting possession while my soul's life remains.

GEORGE ELIOT *Diary*

If 31 December is the day for looking back and assessing the joys and ills the year brought, then 1 January is the time to look ahead. Here are some diverse New Year thoughts.

1785

WHETHER this be the last or no, may it be the best year of my life!

JOHN WESLEY *Diary*

1792

I BREAKFASTED, dined, &c. again at home. Nancy breakfasted, dined, &c. again at home. I read Prayers and Preached this Afternoon at Weston Church. None from Weston-House at Church.

Pray God an happy Year may this be to us and to all our Friends every where, and Especially to our most worthy and particular Friend Mrs Custance, now under very great Affliction: may thy Almighty Goodness O Lord! send thy restoring Angel to her and bless every medicine made use of for her recovery: And also send Comfort to her truly most most affectionate and loving Husband Mr Custance in his present great distress, and to their dear Children Health.

JAMES WOODFORDE *The Diary of a Country Parson*

1832

SUNDAY. I suppose I must go on here with my diary – as I can't get another book.

This is the first day of a new year; and I am not in the humour for being wished a happy one. Into thy hands oh God of all consolation, into thy merciful hands which chastise not willingly I commit the remains of my earthly happiness; and Thou mayest will that from these few barley loaves & small fishes, twelve basketfuls may be gathered.

ELIZABETH BARRETT *Diary*

I SAT up last night to watch the old year out and the new year in. The Church bells rang at intervals all last night and all today. At 6 I went to Crafta Webb to begin my cottage lectures there. It was raining fast when I started, but when I got as far as the Common I noticed that the ground was white. At first I thought it was moonlight. Then I saw it was snow. At Crafta Webb the snowstorm was blinding and stifling, and I passed by Preece's cottage where I was going to hold the lecture without seeing it in the thickness of the driving snow. Before the lecture I went in to see old John Williams. On opening the door I was confronted by the motionless silent figure of a person veiled and wearing a conical cap which I presently discovered to be a dead pig hanging up by its snout. John Williams deplored my being out in such a night and said it was not fit for me. There were not many people at the service but the usual faithful few When I came back the storm was worse and so thick and driving that I was glad I was between hedges and not out on the open hill. The young people at the servants' party seemed to be enjoying themselves with dancing and singing. After supper they came into the dining-room to sing to me each with a comical cap out of a cracker on her head. Then there was a snapdragon and they went away about 10.30.

FRANCIS KILVERT *Diary 1870–1879*

NOW WHEN Jesus was born in Bethlehem of Judea in the days of Herod the king, behold, there came wise men from the east to Jerusalem.

2 Saying, Where is he that is born King of the Jews? for we have seen his star in the east, and are come to worship him.

THE BIBLE *St Matthew 2*

❧ ❧

The sixth of January is Twelfth Night, the feast of Epiphany, when the three Magi came bearing gifts to Jesus. On this day all the trappings of Christmas, the holly and the ivy, the paper chains, the Christmas tree and the garland on the front door should be removed. The children are sad about this, but most housewives are secretly relieved to see the home in its usual, more sober aspect.

WE THREE kings of Orient are,
Bearing gifts we traverse afar,
Field and fountain, moor and mountain,
Following yonder star.

O star of wonder, star of night,
Star with royal beauty bright,
Westward leading, still proceeding,
Guide us to thy perfect light.

JOHN HENRY HOPKINS *We Three Kings of Orient Are*

TWELFTH NIGHT

No night could be darker than this night,
no cold so cold,
as the blood snaps like a wire,
and the heart's sap stills,
and the year seems defeated.

O never again, it seems, can green things run,
or sky birds fly,
or the grass exhale its humming breath
powdered with pimpernels,
from this dark lung of winter.

Yet here are lessons for the final mile
of pilgrim kings;
the mile still left when all have reached
their tether's end: that mile
where the Child lies hid.

For see, beneath the hand, the earth already
warms and glows;
for men with shepherd's eyes there are
signs in the dark, the turning stars,
the lamb's returning time.

Out of this utter death he's born again,
his birth our saviour;
from terror's equinox he climbs and grows,
drawing his finger's light across our blood –
the sun of heaven, and the son of God.

L A U R I E L E E

6 January 1663

MYSELF somewhat vexed at my wife's neglect in leaving of
her scarfe, waistcoat, and nightdressings in the coach today
that brought us from Westminster, though I confess she did
give them to me to look after – yet it was her fault not to see
that I did take them out of the coach. This night making an
end wholly of Christmas, with a mind fully satisfyed with the
great pleasures we have had by being abroad from home.
And I do find my mind so apt to run its old wont of pleasures,
that it is high time to betake myself to my late vows, which I
will tomorrow, God willing, perfect and bind myself to, that
so I may for a great while do my duty, as I have well begun,
and encrease my good name and esteem in the world and
get money, which sweetens all things and whereof I have
much need.

SAMUEL PEPYS *Diary*

As we go to bed on 6 January we know that Christmas is over. Tomorrow, things are back to the daily routine.

We have had our fun, renewed friendships, looked back on the follies and fears of the past year and toasted the new one, intending to profit by our experiences.

Christmas has shown us, yet again, that hope still shines in a dark world, and perhaps Cardinal John Newman's prayer sums it up.

MAY EACH Christmas, as it comes, find us more and more like Him who at this time became a little child, for our sake, more simple-minded, more humble, more affectionate, more resigned, more happy, more full of God.

CARDINAL JOHN NEWMAN

And, as Tiny Tim says:

"God bless us everyone!"

ACKNOWLEDGMENTS

Extract from *Corduroy* by Adrian Bell reprinted by permission of the author's estate.

Extract from "Christmas" by John Betjeman is reproduced by permission of John Murray (Publishers) Ltd.

Extract from *The Diaries of Noël Coward*, edited by Graham Payn and Sheridan Morley, is reproduced by permission of George Weidenfeld & Nicolson Ltd.

Extract from "The Christmas Tree" from *The Complete Poems of C. Day Lewis* (Sinclair-Stevenson Ltd, London, 1992).

"Christmas Stocking" from *The Children's Bells* (Oxford University Press) and "This Holy Night" from *Silver, Sand and Snow* (Michael Joseph Ltd) by Eleanor Farjeon are reprinted by permission of David Higham Associates Ltd.

"Twelfth Night" by Laurie Lee reprinted by permission of the Peters Fraser & Dunlop Group Ltd.

Extract from *If I May* copyright 1920 by A.A. Milne, reproduced by permission of Curtis Brown Ltd, London.

Extract from *The Last Grain Race* by Eric Newby is reprinted by permission of Martin Secker & Warburg Ltd.

Extract from *The Tailor of Gloucester* by Beatrix Potter copyright © Frederick Warne & Co., 1903.

Extracts from *Drawn from Memory* copyright 1957 E.H. Shepard, reproduced by permission of Curtis Brown Ltd, London, and Methuen London.

Extracts from *A Child's Christmas in Wales* (Dent) by Dylan Thomas are reproduced by permission of David Higham Associates.

Every effort has been made to contact copyright holders, and the publishers would be interested to hear from any copyright holders not here acknowledged.